15.00

# FEATHER
# TALES

# Sandy Sea Gull

David M. Sargent, Jr., and his friends live in Northwest Arkansas. His writing career began in 1995 with a cruel joke being played on his mother. The friends pictured with him are (from left to right), Vera, Buffy, and Mary.

Dave Sargent is a lifelong resident of the small town of Prairie Grove, Arkansas. A fourth-generation dairy farmer, Dave began writing in early December, 1990. He enjoys the outdoors and has a real love for birds and animals.

# Sandy Sea Gull

By

## Dave Sargent

Illustrated by
Jane Lenoir

Ozark Publishing, Inc.
P.O. Box 228
Prairie Grove, AR 72753

Library of Congress cataloging-in-publication data

Sargent, Dave, 1941—
 Sandy Sea Gull / by Dave Sargent ; illustrated
by Jane Lenoir.
 p. cm.
 Summary: When an unexpected flood threatens
Farmer John's place, Sandy Sea Gull watches her new
friend Billy Beaver work to divert the waters and save
the farm. Includes nonfiction information on gulls.
 ISBN 1-56763-457-5 (cloth) ISBN 1-56763-
458-3 (pbk.)
 [1 Gulls--Fiction. 2. Beavers--Fiction.] I.
Lenoir, Jane, 1950- ill. II. Title.

PZ7.S2465 San 2000
[Fic]--dc21

99-059546

Printed in the United States of America

# Inspired by

my many trips to the ocean, walking along the beach, watching and listening to the sea gulls.

# Dedicated to

all students who have vacationed or lived near an ocean and watched or listened to sea gulls.  It seems they are always busy diving for food. They work for everything they eat.

# Foreword

When an unexpected flood threatens Farmer John's Place, Sandy Sea Gull watches her new friend, Billy Beaver, work his heart out trying to divert the flood waters and save the farm.

# Contents

# Sandy Sea Gull

If you would like to have an author of The Feather Tale Series visit your school, free of charge, just call 1-800-321-5671 or 1-800-960-3876.

# One

## The Cherry Tree

Palm trees swayed with the gentle movement of the warm ocean breeze. Sandy Sea Gull gazed down the beach, hoping to see old friends or something new and interesting. The shoreline was void of activity with the exception of a lone crab who was digging a hole in the wet sand. I am so bored! she thought as she watched the crab disappear beneath a small mound of seaweed.

"I am going to improve my day today by traveling," Sandy muttered.

"Perhaps I will see new country and meet a new friend."

Several hours later, Sandy was gliding over tall trees and fresh water lakes and rivers.

The black feathers on Sandy's head glistened beneath the rays of the hot sun as she soared northward. Her gray and white body shivered with excitement as her eyes scanned the land for adventure.

Suddenly the sound of angry voices captured Sandy's attention, and she flew lower, circling and observing the disturbance.

"Dadburnit! Who did this? Just who in tarnation cut down my cherry tree?" Farmer John bellowed. "Somebody answer me! Who in the world did this terrible thing? Why, I planted that sapling a long time ago for Molly to make some cherry jelly. Just look at it! The poor thing's been cut into a million little pieces! Now! I wanna know! Just who in the cat-hair did this?"

Sandy Sea Gull noticed a critter hustling away from the scene of the tree trimming crime. She landed on the branch of a tree above him.

"Mercy!" she heard the furry critter grumble. "What a grouch!"

Sandy cocked her head to one side and glared down at him.

"You would be a grouch, too," she responded, "if someone chopped down your cherry tree."

The furry critter quickly looked to his right. Then he jerked his head to the left. He turned around and looked, but now his back was arched as though ready to run.

"I'm up here," Sandy said with a chuckle.

As the little fellow glanced upward, Sandy Sea Gull glided down to the ground beside him. He backed up several paces and stared at her, then snorted, "I see nothing wrong with chopping down trees. It's what I do best!"

"What is your name?" Sandy asked.

"Billy Beaver," the little critter said with a big smile. His two front teeth glistened white against his furry brown face, and he slapped his paddle-like tail on the ground to emphasize his pride in his heritage.

"Well, Billy Beaver, my name is Sandy Sea Gull, and I am here to tell you that it is much better to be a friend to others than to be an enemy. Being an enemy," she added in a deeper tone of voice, "or a goose-bite is a very dangerous and lonely way to live."

"Aw," Billy squeaked, "I was just having some fun."

"Well," Sandy declared in a loud voice, "I think you better stop having so much fun and start . . ."

Voices from the area of the bedraggled remains of the cherry tree interrupted the two.

"I hate to do it," Farmer John said, "but, Molly, I gotta get rid of that pesky beaver if we're ever going to raise fruit crops. He gets rid of them faster than I can plant them!"

Sandy watched the woman nod her head in agreement.

"You're right, John," she said quietly. "I like beavers, but this one is not our friend."

"Nope, he's not a friend," John growled. "As a matter of fact, this one is about to become our enemy. I don't know what else to do, Molly. Go get a trap, and I'll try to catch him. We've got to take care of this problem before that little fellow does more damage."

# Two

## The Unexpected Flood

As the man and woman turned to leave, Sandy looked at Billy with a concerned expression on her face.

"What's wrong?" he asked. "You look worried."

"I am," Sandy murmured. "Do you know what a trap is used for?"

Billy giggled and scratched at the ground with his front paw.

"Well, of course I know what an old trap is used for," he snickered. "That's what folks use to catch small fish. It has nothing to do with me."

Sandy groaned and shook her head. She patted one foot on the ground as though losing her patience with the young beaver. I have to explain, she silently decided, or he will never understand the seriousness of the situation.

"Okay, Billy, you are right," she agreed. "Traps are used to catch small fish. But they are also used to catch ornery beavers who chop down cherry trees."

Sandy watched Billy's smile fade into a worried frown, but before she had a chance to explain, a loud boom echoed across the land. Billy jumped in terror, and his teeth began to chatter. The sky suddenly became dark, and rain started to pelt down. A lightning bolt streaked across the dark sky, followed by a second loud

rumble of thunder. The gull and the
beaver quickly took refuge beneath
the dense foliage.

"Maybe this storm will take Farmer John's mind off trapping for ornery beavers," Billy snorted. "But the rain doesn't usually last long."

Three hours later, the deluge of rain continued, and water poured forth over the land in huge rivers. Sandy Sea Gull and Billy Beaver watched the torrential downpour sweep away the remnants of the cherry tree. Additional strikes of lightning and earth-shaking booms of thunder convinced the bird and beaver that this storm was not over.

Suddenly Sandy noticed the water growing deeper, and she gasped.

"Billy," she yelled. "It looks like the farm is going to be flooded. Can we prevent this farmer and his family from being washed away?"

Billy looked at the huge river of water that was rising rapidly toward the farmhouse. He thought of Farmer John and Molly and their three little girls.

"Yes," he called to Sandy. "I think I can build a dam on the south side of the barn, and it should divert the water around the farmhouse."

Sandy tried to keep up with the busy beaver as he quickly ran toward a grove of trees. He gnawed through the trunk of the first tree in record time. It hardly had time to fall to the ground before the little critter was eating his way through another one.

Sandy watched as the expert engineer of flood control worked feverishly throughout the night. He chewed, gnawed, and positioned the fallen trees into a large dam.

In the pre-dawn hours, the lightning and thunder moved on and the rain subsided into a light mist. Barney the Bear Killer came out of his side shed, stretched and then looked all around, surveying the high water and the mound of trees.

Barney had watched Billy off and on during the long night. Now he climbed to the top of the mound and sniffed, then started out on his early morning rounds.

As the sun slowly ascended on the eastern horizon, Sandy Sea Gull saw that the water had been diverted around the farmhouse, barn, and out-buildings of Farmer John's Place. And then she spotted young Billy sound asleep atop the enormous dam of trees. His little cheeks and mouth quivered with each exhaled snore.

Sandy smiled as she perched on a branch near his head. "I'm so proud of you, Billy Beaver," she murmured. "Surely Farmer John will be your friend now."

# Three

## Billy's Dam Saves the Farm

One hour passed quietly and quickly as Sandy Sea Gull stood like a sentry over the exhausted little beaver. She heard the barnyard rooster crow as the sun peeked through the thin layer of clouds that were rapidly dispersing overhead.

"I hope," she muttered quietly, "that Farmer John realizes how hard Billy Beaver has worked. He put his heart and soul into saving this farm."

The sea gull glanced at the remaining trunks of the grove of trees and groaned, "Oh my, I hope there weren't any cherry trees among them. That would most certainly be a sad twist of fate!"

Suddenly the sound of voices interrupted her negative train of thought. Uh oh, she mused. I think Farmer John and Molly are coming this way. Oh, dear! I better wake Billy Beaver before they see him. What if they get mad when they see the trees cut down and piled in a big heap? Farmer John may get so mad that he shoots Billy.

Sandy nudged Billy on the nose with her beak, but he didn't waken. She put her foot on his forehead and tried to open his eyes, but the young beaver continued snoring quietly. Finally she tickled Billy's nose with one wing feather, and he sneezed.

As Billy slowly opened one eye, Sandy spotted the man and woman walking through the muddy field toward them.

"Come on, Billy," she scolded. "Farmer John is coming. We have to get out of here!"

Billy sat up and rubbed his eyes with one paw. Sandy Sea Gull was dancing back and forth on the tree limb as Billy yawned and stretched.

"Billy! Get up!" she screamed.

Again, Sandy glanced toward Farmer John. He had stopped and was standing there, staring at the massive pile of trees. He took off his hat before wiping his brow on his shirt sleeve.

"Look Molly," he said in a calm voice, "I can't believe this. Do you see what I see?"

Molly nodded and wiped a tear from her cheek as she murmured, "Yes, John. I see that the little beaver who chopped down your cherry tree also saved our farm."

"I reckon he did," Farmer John said as he slipped his arm around Molly's shoulders. "And he did it by clearing the land of the trees that I was going to have to cut down next spring. That little fellow is a good friend to us, Molly. I guess one cherry tree is a small amount to pay for all of the good he did last night."

"Psst," Sandy whispered. "Come on, Billy. Let's leave now. I don't think they have seen you yet."

Billy scurried down the pile of

trees and ran into the woods beyond the field. Sandy glided silently above his head until he came to rest beside a tree. He was puffing and panting as she landed beside him.

"Billy," Sandy said quietly, "you are a remarkable young beaver. And," she added proudly, "I'm glad that you are my friend!"

Billy scuffed at the wet ground with one paw and grinned.

"I'm proud that you're my friend, Sandy," he stuttered. "I didn't realize how important friendship was until I got in that mess over the silly cherry tree. It feels real good to make folks happy. As a matter of fact," he added with a grin, "I think Farmer John is a friend of mine and mighty proud of my tree trimming now. Don't you?"

"Yes," Sandy murmured. "I think he is, but you must try to be careful to be kind to friends and to choose the right trees to cut down. As you found out last night, an irate friend is pretty close to being an enemy."

"I'll be careful," Billy promised. "And I'm going to try to meet more friends in the woods. Maybe they could use a little of my help, too!"

Sandy grinned and winked. "I'm sure that most critters could use a good friend like you. Now I must go," she said. " I have many miles to travel before I'll see any of my old friends. Good-by, Billy Beaver."

A short time later, the sea gull was soaring high above the tree tops. Her heart was singing at the success of her venture. And, she mused, I am proud of my new beaver friend. I just hope that he stays away from cherry trees. And apple trees and pear trees and . . . . Hmmm . . .

# Four

## Gull Facts

*Gull* is a common name for approximately 47 species of long-winged, web-footed seabirds, the most familiar birds of the seashore. The commonly used name *sea gull* is a misnomer. Many species nest or feed inland, and most of the rest are strictly coastal; only the kittiwakes are truly oceanic during the non-breeding season.

Gulls are distributed world-wide, excluding only tropical deserts and jungles, the central Pacific islands, and most of Antarctica. Some gulls migrate.

Gull sizes, from bill to tail, range from 27 to 80 cm (11 to 31 in). The bill is hooked. Except for the totally white ivory gull, the birds vary from pale gray to black above, and from white to gray below. The heads of many have black, gray, or dark brown hoods during breeding season. Many of the gray-winged species have black or darker gray wing tips, often with white spots. The sexes are alike in color.

Young gulls have mottled brown or gray plumage, taking as long as four years (in the larger species) to attain the definitive adult coloration through a progressive series of annual molts.

Gulls are equipped for versatility rather than specialization. For example, their wings are good for soaring as well as for strong and agile powered flight, but they cannot use air currents as efficiently as albatrosses or fly as fast as falcons.

Gulls' foraging includes fishing, scavenging, preying on eggs, catching insects, following plows for earthworms and ships for garbage, dropping shellfish from a height to break them open, and paddling feet to stir up organisms in shallow water.

Gulls breed colonially, mostly on the flat ground of beaches, marshes, or riverbeds, where they build simple, shallow, grass-lined nests. Several species nest on ledges of cliffs, notably the kittiwakes. The clutch consists of two or three green-ish-brown, speckled eggs, which take 20 to 30 days to incubate. At hatching the chicks have down feathers, and the eyes are open.

Chicks can stand but are dependent on their parents for food and warmth. The parents share in incubating the eggs and in brooding and feeding (by regurgitation) the chicks, which fledge between four and six weeks after hatching. Gulls have been known to live as long as 40 years in captivity and as long as 36 years in the wild.

Territory defense, pair formation, parent-chick interactions, and other gull activities involve communication behavior consisting of postures, movements, and calls, some of which are quite complex both in form and in function. For example, courting gulls perform threat displays, but they do so in sequences that apparently modify the meaning of the display. Recognition of one individual by another by such means has been demonstrated experimentally. Pair bonds may be long lasting.

Gulls may thrive at the expense of other species. For example, larger gulls are known to drive out smaller gulls and terns from nesting territories, partly through egg and chick predation. Gulls' scavenging can also affect the ecology of urban environments. Airfields (and the garbage dumps that are commonly located near them) attract large numbers of gulls, which present a collision hazard to aircraft; this problem has yet to be solved. In some places, gulls' eggs are collected for food.

J
Sargent